# No Turtle Stew Today

An African tale told by Anne Adeney

Illustrated by Giuliano Ferri

W

FRANKLIN WATTS

LONDON•SYDNEY

First published in 2010 by
Franklin Watts
338 Euston Road
London
NW1 3BH

Franklin Watts Australia
Level 17/207 Kent Street
Sydney
NSW 2000

A CIP catalogue record for this book is available
from the British Library.

ISBN 978 0 7496 9419 7 (hbk)
ISBN 978 0 7496 9425 8 (pbk)

**Series Editor:** Jackie Hamley
**Editor:** Melanie Palmer
**Series Advisor:** Catherine Glavina
**Series Designer:** Peter Scoulding

Printed in China

Franklin Watts is a division of
Hachette Children's Books,
an Hachette UK company.
www.hachette.co.uk

This tale comes from
Africa. Can you find
this on a map?

Long ago, turtles lived
only on land.

"I'm hungry!" said Bayo, an African chief.

"Fetch me some food!"
he ordered his men.

So the men went hunting ...
and caught a big turtle.

They took it to the chief.
"Good!" said Bayo.
"Let's have turtle stew."

But Turtle was clever and
did not want to be eaten.

"You'll have to kill me first and remove my shell," he told them.

"We'll break it with sticks," said the hunters.

"My shell is too hard
to break," said Turtle.

15

16

"Why not throw me in
the river and drown me?"
he told Bayo.

"Good idea!" said Bayo.
"Drown the turtle, then
we will eat him."

18

19

The hunters threw Turtle
into the river and waited.

Later, Bayo said,
"I'm hungry! Isn't that
turtle drowned yet?"

Then Turtle floated up
and popped his head
out of his shell.

23

"Foolish people!" he cried.
"Put your cooking pot away.

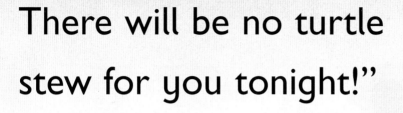

There will be no turtle
stew for you tonight!"

The clever turtle swam off, saying, "I'll live in water from now on. It is much safer!"

And that is just what
Turtle did.

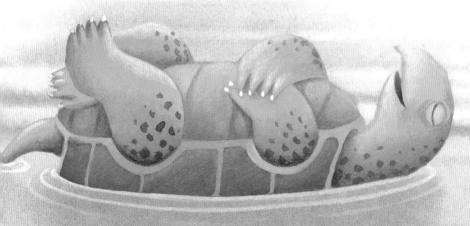

# Puzzle 1

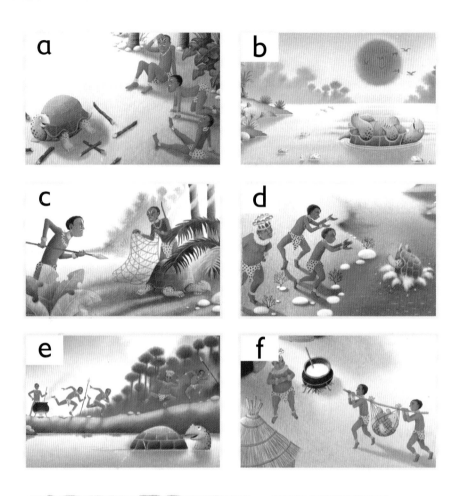

Put these pictures in the correct order.
Now tell the story in your own words.
What different endings can you think of?

# Puzzle 2

cunning   scared
proud

impatient   kind
angry

clever   foolish
annoyed

Choose the correct words for each character. Which words are incorrect? Turn over to find the answers.

# Answers

## Puzzle 1

The correct order is: 1c, 2f, 3a, 4d, 5e, 6b

## Puzzle 2

**Turtle**: the correct words are cunning, proud

The incorrect word is scared

**Bayo**: the correct words are angry, impatient

The incorrect word is kind

**Hunters**: the correct words are foolish, annoyed

The incorrect word is clever

### Look out for more Leapfrog World Tales:

**Chief Five Heads**
ISBN 978 0 7496 8593 5*
ISBN 978 0 7496 8599 7

**Baba Yaga**
ISBN 978 0 7496 8594 2*
ISBN 978 0 7496 8600 0

**Issun Boshi**
ISBN 978 0 7496 8595 9*
ISBN 978 0 7496 8601 7

**The Frog Emperor**
ISBN 978 0 7496 8596 6*
ISBN 978 0 7496 8602 4

**The Gold-Giving Snake**
ISBN 978 0 7496 8597 3*
ISBN 978 0 7496 8603 1

**The Bone Giant**
ISBN 978 0 7496 8598 0*
ISBN 978 0 7496 8604 8

**Bluebird and Coyote**
ISBN 978 0 7496 9415 9*
ISBN 978 0 7496 9421 0

**Anansi the Banana Thief**
ISBN 978 0 7496 9416 6*
ISBN 978 0 7496 9422 7

**Brer Rabbit and the Well**
ISBN 978 0 7496 9417 3*
ISBN 978 0 7496 9423 4

**Little Tiger and the Fire**
ISBN 978 0 7496 9418 0*
ISBN 978 0 7496 9424 1

**No Turtle Stew Today**
ISBN 978 0 7496 9419 7*
ISBN 978 0 7496 9425 8

**Too Many Webs for Anansi**
ISBN 978 0 7496 9420 3*
ISBN 978 0 7496 9426 5

*hardback